Compatible with

IX AGE™

The 9th Age™

Beauty and Terror

Impressum:

Written by the T9A Team

Published by FlorianGressConsulting, Rosenweg 24, 93053 Regensburg, Germany

Printed by Amazon Media EU S.à r.l., 5 Rue Plaetis, L-2338, Luxembourg

ISBN: **978-3-9824212-2-3**

THE IX AGE
FANTASY BATTLES

A 9TH AGE SUPPLEMENT

DREAD ELVES
BEAUTY AND TERROR

THE IX AGE
FANTASY BATTLES

A 9TH AGE SUPPLEMENT

DREAD ELVES
BEAUTY AND TERROR

Lead authors: Daniel Eugui, Scott Jones

Faction leader: Marko Lukić

Head of Background: Edward Murdoch

Contributing authors: Henry P Miller, Alessandro Vivaldi

Editing: John Wallis

Layout: Kacper Bucki

First Edition 04/2021

POST-MISSION REPORT – INQ FIRST CLASS ELMAR LORCA

RATED SUB-ROSA – FOR GENERAL STAFF

948 AS, Damos 27th

The prevailing situation in Avranne is one of severe battle damage. The forces of the Republic of Dathen have inflicted thorough destruction, and the town has suffered an exodus of refugees into the surrounding hills, straining the local infrastructure. Edmund Readwalde, the Earl of Avranne, has accepted the offer of Imperial aid. I believe this is in part to hasten a response from the Equitan court, where the Earl is out of favour (local source). We judge that his cooperation with Aschau is an attempt to leverage the Crown's paranoia about Imperial motives in the region. We advise maintaining this approach.

The raid employed typical Daeb tactics. Eyewitnesses reported a sudden, impenetrable fog from the sea, within which floating masses emerged, approximately the size of houses.

It is likely the elves reconnoitred the city; they displayed uncanny knowledge of the guard's routines, the city's pattern of life and the timing of local tides.

The raid was heralded by forward elements of probable Black Cloak operatives. It is likely these agents were masquerading as merchants in the weeks preceding the raid in order to gather intelligence. Unfamiliar persons claiming to be Arandai (local source) were sighted in the city – however, my contacts among the Highborn merchant fleet claim no knowledge of any individuals fitting their description or their vessel (reliable source).

The action at Avranne is significant because reports of similar suspicious activity on the Imperial coast have been filed in recent weeks, matching patterns described above. Still more troubling, the leader of the Dread Legion which fell upon the town (codename BLACK ROSE) is a Daeb aristocrat of some repute. She is a formidable soldier, having completed conventional military training by choice, but she is even more accomplished in espionage. Current intelligence suggests she may have infiltrated the higher echelons of the Highborn Court prior to her new command. At present, it is not clear who may be under her sway. Our assets within the Aldan diplomatic sphere are briefed on this situation and we anticipate more information soon.

BLACK ROSE is influential within the Senate's Fatherland faction, whose star is rising in Rathaen. This faction presents an existential threat to all of Vetia, and to Sonnstahl most of all. Elven memory is long, and my research suggests many of the senior scions of the Fatherland faction still dwell on their defeat in Vetia at the time of Sonnstahl's founding.

I have briefed my agents in the northern sector to pay close attention to maritime activity. The Inquisition recommends all garrison commanders are ordered to increase vigilance and ensure local infrastructure and services are adequate to support rapid mobilisation.

This matter is now of the highest priority. Please anticipate further reporting. I have enclosed several documents from my wider research that may be of interest.

Sunna libera nos.

E. Lorca

Postscript:
The Earl of Avranne shows promise as an asset to the Inquisition and I recommend careful cultivation.

In early years, great were the fears;
Saurians ruled with claws and spears.
Quell. Compel.

All would fight, through day and night;
To free the races from their plight.
Shred. Behead.

In darkest hour, no ancestor cowered;
Yet ours would demonstrate true power.
Slay. Flay.

No mercy given, to dark deeds driven;
What must be done, needs not forgiven.
Thrive. Survive.

THE DIARY OF A NOBLE ELF OF VIRENTIA

Extracts presented to the Society of Oceanic Exploration by an anonymous benefactor, provenance unknown.

My heart is filled with an incomparable joy and a sense of freedom, as it is whenever I sail the ocean. Perhaps it's my Daeb soul – that doomed connection with the waves and the salt.

In any event, the journey has been pleasant, if long. Three cycles of the moon have elapsed since I embarked on this circuitous path towards Silexian Dathen, leaving those parts of our Republic I call home; those parts that lie on distant shores. The first stage of the journey was calm, as we left Virentian waters and approached the Shattered Sea. But here the protection of Harag proved insufficient to keep our flotilla safe. The storm was as sudden as it was violent; two of our larger ships and three of the smaller escorts were engulfed by the ferocious waters, their elegant and curved hulls unable to endure.

We were driven far out into the Great Ocean. When we made inventory, I was amazed and relieved to find that the main part of my cargo was safe: three hundred and twenty two barrels of fine wine, three full cellars of salted fish and oysters, two hundred and eighty slaves and two beautiful manticores that were promised to a beastmaster in Caen Dracin. Given we had only lost seven slaves who went mad and had to be put down, my mood improved notably.

Today, I have been wandering along the deck of the Chilling Wind, my proud flagship. It is boiling with activity. The corsairs are supervising the repairs, atop the crew's usual duties with the rigging and the sails. The majority are young and headstrong elves; many of them have just left the Academy. But there are also experienced sailors and warriors, matchless readers of Harag's mood in the skies – and equally proficient in gutting their enemies with steel. These veterans are feared and respected by the rest of the crew, with their broad capes made from the hide of sea monsters as a symbol of their status.

I looked out to the nearest ship, the Serpent's Fang. I could see the beast handlers I had hired from one of the finest taming schools to guard the manticores. I was worried about transporting such powerful beasts, but these experts are not to be doubted. Their extraordinary skills of domination are worth every penny.

Filling my lungs with the salty scent of the ocean, I contemplated the waves caressing the hulls of the flotilla. We had lost much time to the storm, but our vessels sailed fast under ship's canvas and slave's oar. At that moment, I felt truly alive.

It had been a long voyage from my home in Virentia. When I finally disembarked in the crowded port of Caen Dracin, I turned in the direction of the angular streets of the city. Before I even took a step, I was approached by a slave, who took me to his master: my cousin and old friend Loraec. He bid me a fair welcome, greeting me with the Daeb salute, right arm across the chest. We headed to a fine balcony where we sat and enjoyed the views of the port and the smell of the ocean.

It had been quite some time since I was last here, I said, and I couldn't help noticing many things had changed.

"I suppose you're right," he replied. "This city is ever crowded, and the constant flow of peoples and goods keeps it changing."

"Your fellow citizens are different from those of my home," I remarked. "There is a striking variety of clothing, hair and customs. The corsairs and youths that sailed with me had their hair shaven at the sides or entirely cropped. Tell me cousin, is this the mark of a cult?"

"Some cults make their followers shave, it is true. But those you have seen are just young idealists craving freedom. You see, when they finish at the Academy, they are no longer obliged to wear their hair in a long braid or mane, as is the old tradition among soldiers. They cut it off to signal their independence, and they start a new path outside the gaze of the state, as corsairs or slavers."

"It sounds to me, my friend, like we are both too old-fashioned to understand."

We finished our drinks and walked from the port to the market, in the center of the city by the fountain of Harag. We continued our conversation, and as I was still intrigued by those young elves, I asked him how the state treated them. This led us to politics.

"There are three major political factions in the Republic," he told me. "We call the first one the Motherland faction. They are mainly descendants of ancient families, those first colonists abandoned and betrayed by their imperial rulers long ago, and now they ever seek to revive the old war with the Highborn and regain the Empire, through military or diplomatic movements. On the other hand, those descendants of the elves that fled Vetia after the wars of the late Golden Age are the core of the Fatherland faction. They see Vetia as our ancestral home, and they want to restore our lands on the continent. These powerful families, from both parties, used to see the young ones you mentioned as upstarts, and paid little attention, but they have grown both in number and in power. Indeed for many centuries, such demagogues and fortune-seekers have formed the third faction, the Slavers, who advocate for accepting the position of strength Dathen has built, and using it to grow more prosperous, rather than chasing after ancient grudges."

As we came closer to the market, I admired the high walls of the inner citadel and the famous statue of Draecarion, a hero of legend long before Dathen gained its independence. Soon the scents and voices of the market were with us, and long rows of slaves marched wearily straight from the port.

"See," my cousin continued. "This is the true wealth of Dathen – the plunder of the whole world. Not some old story about Vetia. Who needs distant lands, when we have the ocean at our fingertips, and the bounty of Silexia at our backs? At least, that's what you'll read in the Slavers' pamphlets."

Come Age of Gold and friends turn cold;
Our time had yet to be foretold.
Bide. Betide.

Brethren haunt the silent wood, donning bow and darkened hood;
Against our kin we, rising, stood.
Waylay. Betray.

Dwarf greed fixate, war propagate
We fought midst peaks and learnt to hate.
Smite. Birthright.

Fate would draw us ever west, cross oceans lay our greatest test;
Break Empire's chains, no more oppressed
Rebel. Deathknell.

Hear this, dwarven scum.

We are the heirs of Aembeghen, founder of our eternal Republic. We don't need tricks, we don't cheat; all of our might is in front of our enemies, for terror is our weapon. We are predators, and predators hunt their prey with honour and without mercy. For you, the honour is to be hunted; you'll need to cheat to escape, for your strength is as nothing before the perfect predators. The mightier you are, the greater our glory.

Do you think threatening me with torture can scare me? We are fear incarnate. We don't fear death, for the Queen of Death is upon us from the moment we are born.

I'm a Siethim of Urlain, and I forsee in his name our victory over your rotten corpses. This land is ours, and our pact with our gods makes it our duty to retake and purge it, erasing your filthy presence.

The Siethims of Nabh will bear the word of bloodthirst among our warriors. The Siethims of Caedhren will select the prey. The Siethims of the Moithir will possess your souls. The Consul of Ceremonies herself will issue a Triumph, in the name of the Aemar, for our field commanders. Dominion is our faith, for the Republic of Dathen is consecrated to the Allfather. In his triple name we declare war, and in battle our blades are guided by his daughter, the Warcrow. Her sons deliver judgement upon the treacherous and the vile.

Incense burns in our temples, slaves are sacrificed, more troops are gathered. The doors of the Temple of Nabh are open: they will not be closed until all of you have met your doom.

The Obsidian Thrones sanctioned this campaign, for it is sacred to all our gods. Members of the Temples, even their High Priests, are leading our troops on the battlefield, guiding their hands, advising our commanders, fulfilling the will of the Gods of the Republic. Victory or death is certain, for a Daeb knows Dathen and the Hall of the Gods are one.

That is all you need to know: you will not be spared. The Phantom Queen will claim your souls. The Stormwitch will favour our fleets. Caedhren will hunt your hopes. Nabh will crush your ambitions as well as your armies. Urlain will sanction victory over your defeated bones and insignias. Our Temples prosper with the fear of our enemies, and the words of your suffering will spread to all Vetia. Human cities will be toppled, dwarven holds will be besieged by terror itself.

This is the alleged taunt issued by Daeb forces of the great Vetian invasion to the dwarves of Nevaz Vanez in hope of luring them to give battle under unfavourable terms. I have considerable reservations that our disgraceful kin would ever be so… verbose, but the insights into the religion and military philosophy do suggest that while the format and style might have been corrupted in reproduction, the content is Daeb.

Observations from our own operatives in Dathen confirm there are two separate institutions: temples and sects. Temples are the sanctioned part of the governmental apparatus, led by Cadhad, Siethim and Rathim; the three main ranks of the priesthood. While some sects operate via official channels within the temple system, others are quite separate, beyond state oversight and control. As is the case in our own noble practices, each deity has several attributes, but a given sect or temple normally focuses on just one. For example, the Allfather is himself three gods in one. Each of these three again takes multiple aspects or specialities. The sect of Yema the Enticer, for example, demonstrates quite different beliefs and practices compared to that of Yema the Bringer of Beauty.

For reference, I have outlined the Daeb Pantheon below – it is identical in most respects to that of the sylvan elves and our own, though the gods are prioritised quite differently. Note that the Divine Twins, as custodians of Wyscan, are worshipped only by the Trewi, while Urlain the Conqueror (called Olaron in the East) enjoys a special reverence in Dathen.

—Extract from the Education Manual for Grey Watcher cadets

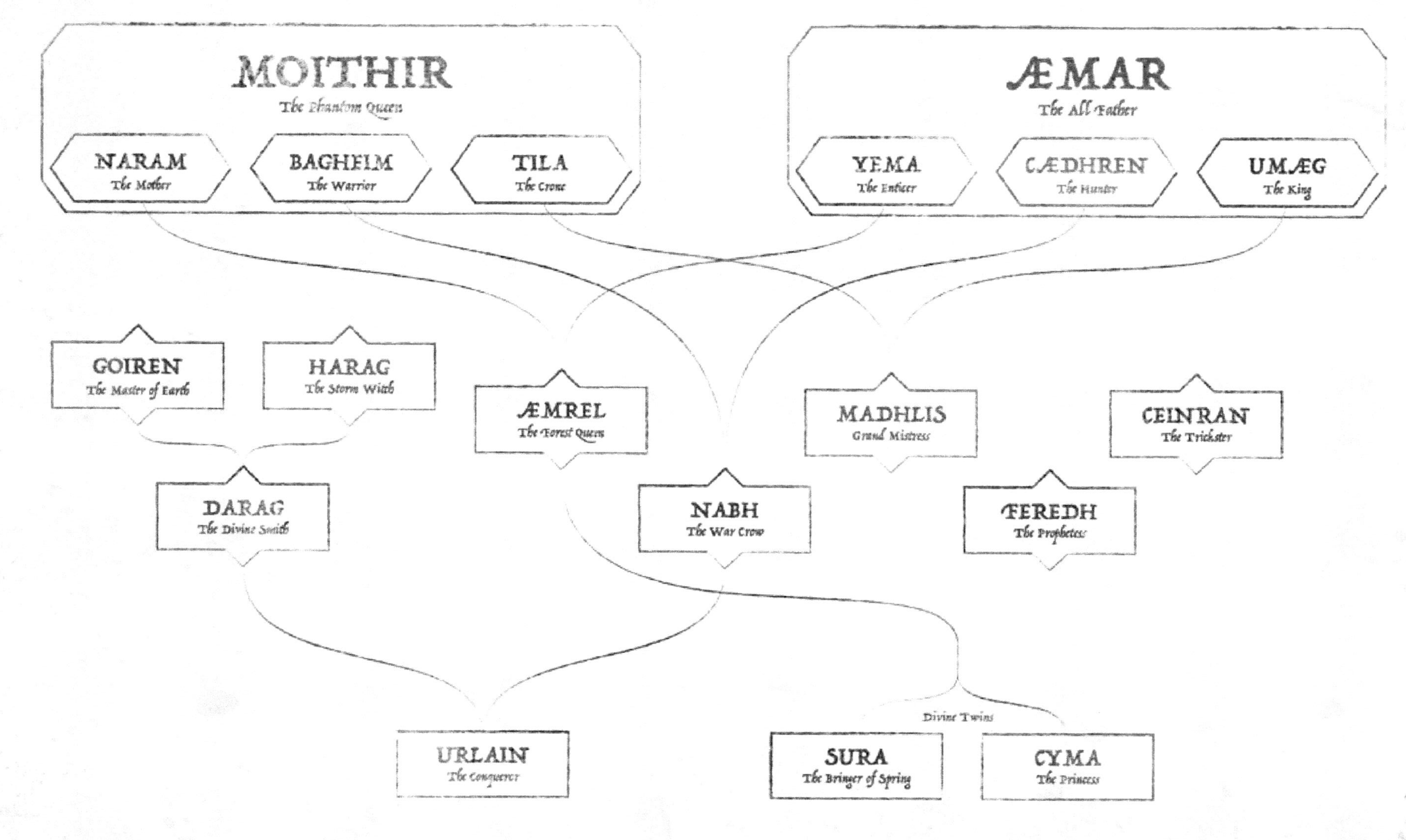

MOITHIR
The Phantom Queen
NARAM
The Mother
BAGHFIM
The Warrior
TILA
The Crone
ÆMAR
The All-Father
YEMA
The Enticer
CÆDHREN
The Hunter
UMÆG
The King
GOIREN
The Master of Earth
HARAG
The Storm Witch
ÆMREL
The Forest Queen
MADHLIS
Grand Mistress
CEINRAN
The Trickster
DARAG
The Divine Smith
NABH
The War Crow
FEREDH
The Prophetess
URLAIN
The Conqueror
SURA
The Bringer of Spring
CYMA
The Princess
Divine Twins

Thus we started our journey towards the ancestral home of my kin, where my cousin and I were raised and taught to be proud citizens of the Republic. The familiar landscapes filled my mind with memories. Long decades had passed since last I cast my gaze on those hills and plains, but they were never forgotten in my heart. The breeze descended from the hills and rippled the wheat where slaves toiled over great, fertile plains, and from afar the broad river Tietha cut the landscape from the horizon to our backs. The water spread broad and mighty as we approached, flowing from the untamed frontiers of the north and west, where the beasts and savages dwell, to the estuary in the east, home of civilisation.

As we continued our journey, we passed through half a dozen fine estates, dominating the surrounding fields. The sound of blades in training and the orders shouted by senior officers proclaimed the strength of the Silexian heartland, and offered a dire warning to the enslaved. The memories of my formation in the Academy came to my mind. I can hardly recall when the magistrate took me to the barracks along with the other youngsters, but the extremities of the training I remember well. This is our contract with the state: fight for the Republic and earn the honour of citizenship. Seeing the latest recruits made me think back to one of my proudest moments, when my seniors voted for me to join the Republic as a legionary.

My cousin jolted me from my reverie, asking about my vineyards back home. I replied that this year's vintage would be a good one.

"I have brought a dozen of my best bottles for you, just as sweet and sophisticated as we Daeb."

"I'd rather drink water like the slaves," he replied, and we both laughed.

I asked him about his plantations, and he began to boast how his four estates were thriving; his last raid to Taphria was a success, and that had allowed him to expand his territory in the west and improve the defenses along its hinterland frontier. He'd even obtained an exploitation license for a coal mine in the east; but this would require more slaves still.

"See," he continued, "the slaves you see in these fields are not suitable for the mines. I need more robust specimens, but not so large that they can't carry rocks through the tunnels. Orcs could fit, even beasts if I cut out their horns, but not anything bigger than that. Vermin are best of all – they're not robust, but they're accustomed to a hard life underground.

"Too short-lived," I replied, but he only chuckled.

"When you find yourself in need of slaves, come and speak to me. I'll give you a good price, and I always keep the best quality for my fellow Daeb, none of that riff raff I sell abroad."

A few hours later, we reached his lands. Around us, an ocean of gold stretched over the plains. We approached the only hill for miles, where the fortified house of my childhood stood vigilant. I couldn't help but notice that the wild woods behind it were more distant now than in my youth. My cousin told me that the border had been expanded some years ago, when a large beast horde descended from the mountains and was defeated. Yet there was still a sizeable garrison training in the drill yard when we arrived – this and the recently restored defenses suggested that the conflict was not over.

"Our land lies at the very border of the Republic," my cousin said. "Here, the conflict never really ends. We must stay sharp. My contacts in the outcast settlements in the woods recently warned me that the barbarians' numbers are growing again. I fear there will be war like we have not seen since our parents' day. You remember?"

I was already lost in memories, from a time I thought I had forgotten.

INTERVIEW TRANSCRIPT – INQ FIRST CLASS ELMAR LORCA

Subject: Fr. Annabelle MUELLER

948 AS, Acrober 1st

Arch Prelate Hildegyth: Are you able to continue?

Fr Annabelle Mueller: Yes, Reverend Mother, I am quite recovered, forgive me.

Hildegyth: There's nothing to forgive, child. Not many escape the Silexian elves; fewer still find themselves back home with the determination to tell their story. Elmar, would you like to begin today?

Inquisitor Lorca: Very well. In your position of a household servant -

Mueller: Slave sir. I was a slave! You don't need to be polite.

Lorca: Quite, my apologies. Now as you were singled out by your mistress for a body-slave, were you privy to anything that would enhance our understanding of their culture?

Mueller: They care for each other. They love and are loved and seem to value life highly. It is sickening to behold, considering the cruelty with which they treat anybody who isn't them. I mean to say those who aren't elves. I often think about my master and mistress's bereavement.

Lorca: Bereavement?

Fr Mueller became visibly upset but refused to adjourn.

Mueller: It was the second year of my captivity. By then, I was like a ghost. All my energy was consumed by avoiding punishment and finding any opportunity to please my masters enough that I could stay in the relative comfort of the house. Field labour would have killed me in a month. That's what they do to you – I come from a proud family, but soon I was like a broken puppy always trying to please them.

It was when the master and mistress's son went off to fight the barbarians, the natives of their lands I think. I remember he was dressed in armour and carrying a shield and spear – there was a celebration. The master and mistress also dressed in armour and there were tears in their eyes. They cry! Can you believe that? It was the same when the son came back from their Academy, just after I arrived at the estate.

Well, this time he was killed. The body was returned to the estate. It was a nasty sight – the corpse was... eviscerated. For my own part I was glad – the youth had been cruel even for a Daeb. He used to practice sword cuts on injured labourers, those who were too damaged to go back to work. If he couldn't slay with the first stroke out of the scabbard, he would rage something awful. Even other elves feared him. But when he died, both master and mistress became inconsolable. They seemed to collapse into each other, and the steward of the estate had to send for an apothecary to administer a calming draught. It was not unseemly for the man of the house to give in to his grief like that, not like it would be in Sonnstahl. The Daeb seem not to care about such concerns.

A pyre was built in their courtyard, and various citizens attended the funeral. The clergy came too - terrifying elven priestesses, one clad in platemail and the other in crimson robes. The priests' attendants and the mistress prepared the body. Almost everyone was dressed in armour – many with spears, and a few with crossbows. Those with bows stood separate, they seemed to be of lower rank. I recognised some of them from everyday chores – it seems that most citizens are also soldiers in Dathen. And not a rabble of fencibles, you understand. They were grim and hard looking like your guardsmen outside.

The funeral started with the armoured priestess who gave some sort of sermon. She led a chant, and everyone replied with shouts and the clattering of weapons. Then the red priestess and her attendants started the pyre. I thought it unusual that all the farm slaves were present; they were made to stand in lines, the temple acolytes behind. The crimson priest seemed to come to a climax…

Fr Mueller again becomes distressed. She takes some brandy.

Hildegyth: Take your time, my girl.

Mueller: All at once, the elvish attendants took out daggers. They…they cut the throats of the farm hands. Their blood was collected… They were being sacrificed, for the dead son.

Fr Mueller continues after collecting herself.

Their blood was collected in vessels and the bodies placed on the pyre. More chants… the clattering of weapons. I was the only adult spared. The mistress made me watch and beat me with her leather switch when I tried to look away, weeping as she did so. She screamed at me to have some respect, and I should blame my human kin for having to witness it. She said there would be a flogging if she was forced to mark my face. I believe this cruelty was how she showed her grief.

They feasted while the pyre burnt the body down to ash. The next morning, the ashes of their son were collected by the priest's attendants. They were put in a jewelled urn and we went to a nearby stream where they were scattered with the blood…there were prayers too. Afterwards, I learnt that the estate had been sold and the master and mistress were moving to one of the cities. The master held the empty urn like a drowning man. That was just before the dark warriors came and we were left free.

Last week, my noble host took me on a hunting party over the borders of his state. Everything was already prepared, and every hunter and slave knew their part. Many of the region's nobles were with us as we marched towards the wilderness, with my cousin and I in the lead. We stopped after a few hours in a clearing in the forest, where the house slaves served breakfast until a scout returned with news of a twelve-point hart. We chased this stag until it turned, my noble host granting me the honour of making the kill, which I did with a sure thrust to its chest.

As the sun set and we were offering the proper libations to Caedhren with the blood of the beast, a strange retinue approached. Half a dozen mounted figures were suddenly visible in the darkness at the edge of the firelight, and everyone turned to my cousin. With a broad knife, he tore one of the legs from the hart and left it on a rock nearby. Three slaves loaded the rest on a cart and the company headed back home in silence.

When we reached the plains again, his mood improved, so I asked him about what had happened. He told me what I had already guessed. The figures we met were acolytes of one of the many outlaw communes that roam the dark woods of the frontier. These lawless, semi-civilized elves are led by mages of terrible power, known as warlocks. The party we met served one such master: a pale witch called the Shadow Maiden. Then my cousin spoke no more.

When we returned to the estate, I questioned a guard about the matter. If he spoke the truth, my cousin had allied with the Shadow Maiden some years ago when he was fighting a great herd of beasts, and since then they had agreed to respect each other's territory. Checking that no one was listening, the guard leaned closer and told me the master was beguiled by the warlock and had planned to marry her. He had been made to see reason just in time – warlocks have a bad reputation, generally loathed by all upstanding Daeb, for they are descended from renegade mages from Celeda Ablan, who refused to submit to or join with the superior Daeb people.

Returning to my chamber, I considered all I had heard of these mysterious frontier communities. It is said they turned to dark arts many ages ago, in the chaos of the Civil War. But they were disowned, first by Aldan, and then by Rathaen, since their experiments had largely targeted our brave rebels. From the White Isles they departed with many magical treasures and tomes that were never vouchsafed to the spellcasting traditions of Dathen. Even now, many warlocks remain even more powerful than temple mages, but such eldritch secrets have addled their appreciation for both civilised society and military strategy, and left them indifferent towards positions of leadership – positions for which they would never be accepted in any case.

Today, it seems the warlocks have found a precarious balance: they are not citizens of Dathen, but they are permitted to settle the borders of its territory. The state watches them closely, and has been known to make use of their power for military purposes when it serves the Republic. There have been marriages with noble families, and exchanges of knowledge and craft-lore with the temples in Rathaen – I had seen warlock-forged blades even in my own lands. Yet despite such faltering exchange, the clear prejudice I had heard in the words of the guard I spoke to proved that most Daeb would never do more than tolerate the presence of these outcasts.

Across the world did spread Death's gloom, many would make for us a tomb;
Yet colonies thrived, enemies died, beasts and men sent to their doom.
Occupy. Purify.

Wealth drew jealous Ablan eyes, donning power's grasping guise;
Upon our lands their troops laid claim, our homes to be their faithless prize.
Secede. Succeed.

In arrogance they stormed our shores, those gleaming toady weakling corps;
For our defiance unprepared; for righteous cause we justly warred.
Ignite. Unite.

We drove them back into the sea, casting out each devotee;
At last this land was ours alone, and we would rule here, truly free.
Ascend. Transcend.

"Good sir, this strong orc slave, just for you? Yes, at a good price. Yours for fifteen pounds of silver – a steal with strong arms like hers. A fighter. She can carry many loads. Orcs are perfect beasts of burden."

"This wretch? I have ten others just like her in my mines already!"

"Not like this one, dwarf. She killed three of my company when she was captured. Threw a javelin clean through a kraken-hide cloak."

"Let me see her. Fifteen pounds, you say? Extortion. Seven is the most I'll give you. And I'm being generous on account of your lost men."

"Seven! These were no 'men' that were killed in taking her. These were hardened elven corsairs with many years on the sea. And she finished three of them."

"Is this true, orc? Speak up!"

"Keep your eyes down, Thing. She's already broken, my friend, and will not answer you – you see the quality of my goods. I only sell the best. She's yours for thirteen. And that's only out of respect for your good taste."

"You elves have no more respect than Lugar's eyebrows. I'll give you a hundred-weight of silk. That's worth fifteen pounds of silver, easy. A tidy sum for a broken beast, wouldn't you say?"

"My dear dwarf, your offer is indeed generous. But the Daeb have no currency but that of silver and flesh. Should I wish for your silk, my ships would simply take it from your warehouses. I want only your coin and your continued custom when we sail through this port again."

—Extract from The Slaver's Tale by Sagarikan dramatist Bhalidastra

As my time in Dathen was coming to an end, my noble cousin insisted I accompany him to the capital, where I could board a ship for my return. We stayed at his town house, and I had a stimulating few days in the ancient city: black stone edifices rising up its inspiring crags, framed in winter months by the legendary oxidised red ice of that monumental, unassailable fjord. I beheld the sights: the great spire of Gar Daecos, seat of power for all Dathen; the enormous Temple of Nabh, dominating the city centre; the extraordinary shrine of Harag, perched on its clifftop like a gnarled old guardian, channeling the power of the Storm. I witnessed the regular sacrifices hurled down into the freezing seas, their ice flows so treacherous to all but the most experienced sailors.

On my last evening, Loraec invited several officers and noble acquaintances to dinner to bid me fare-well. The first guests found us in the library, debating the artistry of the Tetralogies of the Rebellion, an ancient tale from the Ages of Ruin that has long been a favourite for us both. Soon, a varied group had joined the debate, including one Prince Lirain Sialec.

Despite his fearsome military reputation and his menacing visage, he turned out to be very knowledge-able in matters of history. He recited word for word another long poem about the conflict with the Pearl Tyranny, and how the Daeb finally earned our freedom in glorious combat, led by Supreme Legate Aem-beghen, father of our nation. He continued by explaining the role of the cult of Yema – innocent worshi-pers ignorantly persecuted by Aldan, bringing the King of Beauty to our righteous cause, cleansing the White Isles of the true and honest faithful.

Other guests began to chime in, agreeing that the Arandai had lost their way in the Golden Age, before the war. The true Daeb spirit was born in the hardships of the Fatherland, and in the blood and sweat with which we built our home here in the West – while the lofty highborn clung to the luxuries of their towers. We are a people hardened by strife – but these are truisms learned in the crib. Lirain took the lead again, guiding us back to more educated subjects, and everyone fell silent, listening to the famed warrior relating how Rathaen became the great and populated city of today.

When the table was ready, we took our places, and my cousin offered a toast in my honour. The scene was well decorated and ornately furnished, but my attention was held by the calm and mysterious lady seated opposite, regarding me with open curiosity.

"What is your opinion?" The question took me back to reality – I realised I was being addressed by Prince Lirain, seated alongside the woman. Seeing my confusion, he repeated: "I was just telling Lady Gaendra here that Rathaen is disagreeable and chaotic these days. The Temple of Nabh is pressing the Senate to sanction its campaign against the mewling humans in Virentia. What say you?"

I tried to recall what I knew of politics in the capital. Ninety-nine senators, three consuls (crimson for their robes, obsidian for their thrones), three-year terms in each consular office, for a total of nine. All part of the system established by the elders at the end of the war we had just been talking about.

"It is many years since I paid close attention to affairs in Rathaen, I am afraid. I suppose Lady Huraec is in a tough position. She's still the Consul of Ceremony, is she not?"

Lady Gaendra gave me a beguiling smile. "You're better off in ignorance, my friend," she said. "Huraec's already passed through Ceremony and Commerce – she's the Consul of Conflict now. But you're right, she'll have to convince most of the opposing senators if she wants to maintain the support of the Temple. And the favour of the Warcrow is not to be disregarded."

"The Senate would be fools if they sanctioned that campaign," another tall noble said. I would later learn he was a key financier of the Motherland faction. "It's no more than a corsair's raid to my eyes. If we continue down this path, we'll be nothing but looters and pillagers, and we are born to be conquerors. Our true road has always been to dominate the White Isles and all its colonies. The Senate is supposed to serve the people, but I fear it has forgotten our purpose."

At this point, I noticed the discomfort of the figure sitting beside me. My cousin had told me she was lowborn, a hardened veteran who had risen up the ranks of the army. She turned to me and whispered:

"How easy it is to speak for the people when one has had a private tutor and a fine estate on the higher slopes of Rathaen. I wouldn't follow that arrogant twit to battle even if he paid me half the loot, but I would follow Prince Lirain, do you know why? Because he went through the Academy with me, side by side, through every exhausting day of training and every hungry, sleepless night."

The dinner continued late, and the guests departed with their respective retinue and slaves. I stood by the hearth with my cousin Loraec, rambling about all I had seen and learned in my time with him. We Daeb are many things, both here in Silexia as in the colonies, but I had gained an appreciation for that which unites us: whether you are a prince from an ancient dynasty, a commoner or even an exiled outcast, we all have what we take for ourselves, through sheer will – and no Queen, Emperor or God can deny that.

Attention inwards turns and delves, perfecting all our greatest selves;
Weakness to purge, flaws to scourge, and take our place as chief 'mongst elves.
Reject. Perfect.

A Republic stands the test of time, dominion of the maritime;
All assured through pact divine, we seize our destiny sublime.
Consecrate. Venerate.

Our supremacy is now well known, the lesser peoples ours to own;
Bound in chain, broke in will, to kneel before Obsidian Throne.
Dominate. Educate.

Dominating each frontier, to strike by night and disappear;
Dread by name, Dread by will, for us we take the name of Fear.
Prey. Dismay.

—The Rhyme of Dread (trad)

PRIORITY REPORT – INQ FIRST CLASS ELMAR LORCA

RATED SUB-ROSA – FOR GENERAL STAFF

948 AS, Tandemar 22nd

My Lords

Further to my last filing, I must share additional information on the threat from Dathen.

Diplomatic aid from the office of his Eminence the Ambassador from Aldan included intelligence on the dispositions of Daeb naval and military assets. Our own sources, both within the ambassador's residence and the Arandai merchant community, corroborate much of this information. This itelligence included reporting of warbeast specialists mobilising at naval outposts used for launching fleets.

The Arandai operatives emphasise that the capture and mastery of exotic zoological specimens is a central pillar of Daeb culture and military strategy. This brutal discipline is practiced at several dedicated "Taming Schools", where beasts from every corner of the world are brought for "education". The results of these labours are displayed in dramatic arena events for public entertainment, but more worryingly, they can also be used for war.

The reports from Aldan indicate that a large number of specimens from Dathen's "Menagerie" have been assembled for oceanic transport. These include monstrous harpies and hydra, but of greater concern for coastal security are the giant aquatic beasts. Most notable are kraken captured from the Shattered Sea. They are reputed to be capable of slaughtering creatures even larger than themselves and of tearing down harbour walls; their masters are said to possess the ability not only to drive them into battle but also control them once unleashed. Other kinds of oversized squid-like creatures were also observed: beasts constantly shrouded in unnatural mist, said to be able to levitate, with only glimpses of tentacles or teeth seen through the fog. Perhaps this explains something of the Daeb reputation for appearing from nowhere to raid unsuspecting coastlines.

I fear we must take these tales more seriously than we would like. Dathen has won a notable success in the raid on Avranne. It has shown it has the capability to send troops across the Great Ocean and attack Vetia directly. The presence of Obsidian Guard detachments (reliable source) suggests the support of the Senate and the Consuls. This threat of titanic warbeasts should not be underestimated. The prospect of an invasion, at scale, on Imperial soil, cannot be ruled out.

Sunna libera nos

E. Lorca

Postscript:

Source 287 was notably nervous and evasive at debriefing. I felt they were holding back information. I believe this was out of fear rather than an attempt to leverage further funding or advantage from us. This individual will be kept under close surveillance. Compromise cannot be ruled out.

Compatible with
IX
AGE
™
The 9th Age™

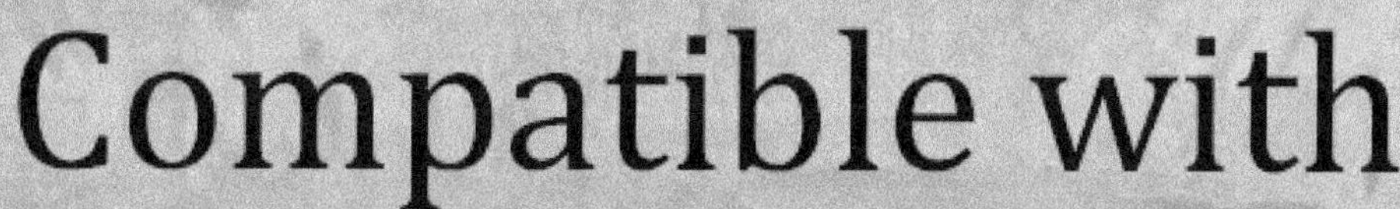

The 9th Age™

THE IX AGE
FANTASY BATTLES

Gather close, ye who would learn of the strange peoples and wondrous places of the Ninth Age. None of us can know the secrets of the entire world, but if you seek a little wisdom on a particular culture or nation, open up this tome and discover what there is to tell.

The Elves of the West? A wise choice – knowing their nature will not spare you blade or chain, but perhaps it will provide a chance to avoid the full wrath of the Dread Elves.

www.ingramcontent.com/pod-product-compliance
Lightning Source LLC
LaVergne TN
LVHW080614200726
843509LV00007B/308